DETECTIVE GODSE

MYSTERY OF KOLLAPUR

ADHYAYAN DATTA RAY

Made with ♥ on the Notion Press Platform
www.notionpress.com

This is presented as a work of fiction and dedicated to nobody.

It is not similar to other detective stories.

This detective story consists of supernatural cases, detective adventures , thriller, suspence etc.

hope you will enjoy it.

Contents

Preface

Hello everyone, first introduce myself. My name is Adhyayan Datta Ray. I am the author of the story " Detective Godse the mystery of Kollapur". From my childhood I wanted to make a story about detective as I was very fond of detective movies, stories, toys etc and when I got to know that Notion Press was giving me a chance to publish my own book then I started to write my own detective story. I was inspired by Nathuram Godse's title (He was the assassin of Mahatma Gandhi. He was a Hindu nationalist from Maharashtra who shot Gandhi in the chest three times at point blank range at a multi-faith prayer meeting in Birla House in New Delhi on 30 January 1948).to make this name Detective Godse as they both have similar title Godse and from my point of view or opinion Godse title sounds like a detective.

Acknowledgements

Thank you Notion Press for giving me this golden chance to publish my book " Detective Godse"and a special thanks to Yamini Shekar, my Publishing Mentor from Notion Press.

Prologue

This story tells about a detective named Detective Godse who is a beginner detective and got his first case which is one of the most dangerous cases ever which is the “Case of Kollapur “. The story tells about the Supernatural problems faced by him on the way to Kollapur and also the mystery of Kollapur .

Foreword

Hello reader, nice to meet you. I first introduced myself. I am the Detective Godse.

Are you ready for the journey to Kolhapur ?

I hope you will like the adventures of this journey.

CHAPTER ONE

Getting the First Case

Hello everyone, first introduce myself. I am the Narrator of this story " The ADR " so, the story starts with the gossiping of many detectives in the" SPY Department "which is a detective department that today a new detective is coming in that department.

One Detective - What is the name of that new detective who is coming ?

Another One - Detective Godse.

Ting ting , the elevator's door opens and the main character of the story enters wearing a brown leather coat, spectacles on his eyes, Rolex watch in his hand, mustache on his face . The Detective Godse.

Godse was not looking as a beginner detective, he was looking as an experienced Onc .

Fourth Wall Breaks

Godse - Hey ! I am not a beginner detective, I have some experience.

Narrator - OK,OK !!

Come to the plot

So, Detective Godse enters the boss room and after seeing detective Godse, Boss directly gives him a case which is “the case of Kollapur “one of the most dangerous cases ever without any conversation .

Boss - This case was taken by 4 detectives but they cannot solve it .

Godse - Ooo, So what about those detectives now ?

Boss - They died or disappeared mysteriously while they were solving the case.

Boss - So do you want to take this case , if you can solve it I will give you promotion to the high level detective.

Boss - So do you ?Yes or no? Do you want to get a promotion or not ?

Godse- Yes, sure. I will.

Boss - There is a challenge , if you solve this case within 7 days I will increase your payment also.

Boss - are you ready to take this challenge ?

Godse - Definitely .

Boss -So, your time starts now.

Godse left the office in a hurry

Boss - I think this time the case will not return to me again.

.

CHAPTER TWO

Nilghum Station Part - 1

Godse bought a train ticket on the way to his house from the office.After reaching his home he saw that the time of the train was 11:50 p.m.So , he started to pack his luggages with some documents of that case that he got from the office when he was coming.When he was going to pack the last document of the case in his luggage, he found that the last document shows the name of the detectives those who were died or being disappear mysteriously while solving the case.There he saw the last detective who was solving the case was detective Arvind one of the famous detective of all time who died solving this case.

Fourth Wall Breaks

Godse - Should I call my boss and tell him that I will not do the case? What do you think should I ?

Godse - No , I will not call my boss because it is a matter of promotion and " Risk Hai To Ishq Hai " and I don't think that I will die .

Come to the Plot

Plot Shifted at night

Time was 11:45 p.m. Godse was ready and waiting at the station for the train then he checked in the railway app on his mobile and he was shocked as the train was one hour late.So he sat with disappointment on a bench nearby him .Suddenly a person looks like a Sadhu sat beside him and he was chanting" Narayana Narayana". he said to Godse not to take any lift of any car .Godse said" who are you ?"and "what are you talking about ".The Sadhu said if you are in trouble then call my name "Narayan Narayan ". Suddenly he heard the sound of a train. When he saw his Watch, 1 hour had passed .

Godse - How could it be possible?

And when he moved his head around again he saw the Sadhu had vanished , he was surprised .

Godse - I think it was my hallucination.

So, he took his luggages with him and got on the train.

Soon , the train started.

CHAPTER THREE

NILGHUM STATION PART - 2

Godse - 5 hours had passed, now the time is 4:50 AM only one station has left. After that I will be in Kollapur .

Five Minutes Later

Godse - Finally,the last station before the Kollapur station comes but suddenly the train stops .

Fourth Wall Breaks

Godse - What kind of thing is going to be happen now ? Do you know ? Any guesses ?

Godse - I also don't know ?

Narrator - But I know ?

Godse - What please tell na.

Narrator - "Aage Aage Dekho hota hai kya", "Picture Abhi Baki Hai Mere Detective".

Come to the Plot

Godse saw the TT outside the compartment of the train. so he go towards him and said that-

Godse - What happened now? Why did the train stop?

TT - Nearby a train accident happened but don't worry no one died.

Godse - How much time is needed to clear that situation?

TT - Don't know but I guess it will take 2 to 3 hours.

Godse - What a pleasant surprise.

Godse - I think today I have bad luck.

Godse - So what can I do in this empty time?

TT - I don't know but I am advising you not to go outside of the station as it is the" Nilgum station".

Godse - What and why ?

TT - I cannot tell the reason to you but I am advising you not to go.Now it is your choice to agree with my words or not.

Godse Didn't obey his word and went outside of the station as he was very curious .

When he went outside he Saw that no one was there and every shop was closed.

Suddenly a man comes from a dark Side and asks Godse if he needs any favour.

Godse - Yes,I am in a hurry and the train has stopped. It will start after 2 to 3 hours so can you get me a car or any vehicle and What is your name ?

The man said my name is Jonathan and I will get you an auto.

Godse - Thank You very much.

Jonathan - Come with me.

Godse went with him to a nearby auto stand.There he saw an auto and two auto drivers were talking to each other.

Jonathan goes there and tells them that a passenger is there .

Then Jonathan talked to me.

Jonathan - where do you want to go ?

Godse - Kollapur.

Jonathan - oh it is too nearby so no money is needed.

Jonathan - Please get in the auto.

Godse - Oh thank you I am very much pleased to you.

The auto started.

CHAPTER FOUR

Nilghum Station Part - 3

5 minutes had passed and Godse got to know the name of that auto driver "Raju ".

Godse - Jonathan.

Jonathan - yes.

Godse - Why was the TT telling me not to go outside of the station ?

Jonathan - Yes because this is one of the famous horror places' ' The Nilghum Station ".

Godse - Why is it horror ?

Jonathan - I am telling you. A very long time ago the Nilgum station was One of the best stations at that time until the new Station master Came .

Godse - What happened when the new station master came ?

Jonathan - Passengers were disappearing mysteriously .

Godse - Why ?

Jonathan - After many investigations police got to know that the new station master named Anil was a serial killer.He was killing the passengers and sold their meat in foreign countries with the help of his two partners.

Godse - After that ?

Jonathan - The police inspector Akhil Kumar spread this news among the villagers and the villagers got ferocious and angry so they planned to kill the station master name Anil and they also got the successed.Anil one of the famous serial killer as well as station master was killed by the villagers of Nilghum.

Godse - So why was it called a haunted place ?

Jonathan - As the spirit of Anil moved in this place and killed the passenger Who came outside of the station.

Godse - Where, in my situation it is not happened yet.

Soon Raju stopped his auto .

When Godse looked outside the auto he Saw that there was a crematorium outside.

When he again saw the inside of the auto there was no one .

Godse - Jonathan, Raju where are you ?

No Response!!

Suddenly he heard the voice of Jonathan who was calling him inside a small forest nearby the crematorium.

He went there in search of Jonathan and Hari.

When he entered that forest ,He saw something that blew up his mind .

He saw many human flesh on the ground, many bones and skulls on the ground and he also saw Raju the auto driver but he didn't have his head. He also met Jonathan who became a partial Skeleton. Blood was coming out of his eyes and he had an axe in his hand and he was giving a creepy smile and started to laugh loudly Ha ha ha ...

Jonathan - I am not Jonathan, I am Anil, one of the most famous serial killers ever, people also know me as the new station master of Nirghum Station.

Jonathan - After a long time I will get some human meat again hahaha...

Godse started running backwards chanting Hanuman Chalisa in fear.

While he was running he could hear the sound of Jonathan and Hari also but he didn't bother .

When he came near the road he saw an old car was coming and a young boy wearing sunglasses in his eyes ,wearing a varsity jacket was driving the car and when the car came close to him the boy said to Godse do you need any help ?

Godse - Yes, I need a lift

The boy said yes sure , get up in the car and Godse in fear get into that car.

Soon the car started.

CHAPTER FIVE

CREMATORIUM

The boy said to Godse " Are you afraid of something ?"

Godse - Yes, as I saw the ghost of Anil Who was a killer and the station master of Nirghum and his one partner Raju..

The boy said to Godse that they are not the ghost of Anil and Hari, they are some people of Nilgum who pretend to be ghosts and prank the passenger who came outside of the station.

Godse - So what about those human flesh , bones and skulls.

the boy said " Oh that are gummy not real ".

Godse felt some sort of relaxment .

Godse - What is your name, boy ?

The boy said "Ravi".

Ravi - What is your name ?

Godse - " Godse ".

Ravi - what are you doing here in this crematorium at 6:00 a.m. ?

Fourth Wall Breaks

Godse - Lets have some fun with this young boy.

Godse - What do you think ? let's do it.

Come to the Plot,Prank Time

Godse - It is my home.

Ravi - what does that mean ?

Godse - Now I am going to watch a movie with my friends.

Ravi - In this early morning. Did you think the theatre should be open ?

Godse - I can enter the theatre whether it is close or not.

Ravi - why is this theatre yours ?

Godse - no.

Ravi - then ?

Godse - Leave it.

Godse - Just play a song for me .

Ravi obeyed his words and played a melodious 90's song by Kishore Kumar .

Godse - Oh what a great song my wife and I danced to in this song before.

Ravi - Before why ? Why not now ?

Godse - Due to death.

Ravi - oh I am very much sorry that is why you went to the crematorium for your wife's death

Godse - Why are you killing my wife? She is still alive.

Ravi - Few minutes ago you said that you went to the crematorium for your wife's death.

Godse - My wife's death, death of mine.

Godse started laughing loudly to pretend to be a ghost to him.

Ravi also started laughing loudly.

Ravi - so your friends means gang of ghosts are going to watch a movie in the theatre hahaha...

Godse - Why ? Ghosts don't have the freedom to watch movies ?

Ravi - Yes sure and gives a creepy smile on his face and started laughing loudly hahaha like a real ghost.

Suddenly Godse saw the Jonathan and Raju in the back seat of the car and they were also laughing loudly like Ravi.

There he got to know that Ravi was the another partner of Jonathan.

Godse -"Mere toh L Lagaye".

Ravi also became a partial skeleton and blood were coming from his mouth.

He grabbed the neck of Godse tightly.

At that time Godse got reminded about that Sadhu who told him not to take any lift of a car and if he would be in trouble then call his name " Narayan Narayan "so, He did the same thing and called his name" Narayan Narayan" after that Godse became senseless.

When he opened his eyes again he found him in front of that crematorium.

CHAPTER SIX

MYSTERY OF KOLLAPUR PART- 1

When Godse saw his watch the time was 7:00 AM .

Godse - Oh no ! One day is almost wasted by me. Only few distance is left to reach Kolhapur so it is better to walk

Godse - If I start to walk from now , I will reach Kollapur in 20 to 30 minutes.

After 25 minutes

Godse - Finally after much trouble, I reached Kollapur.

At first he went to the famous and haunted palace of Kollapur which was' ' Chandra Kateera".

There he got to know that in the ground floor of that Palace was an old man named " Ramu Chacha" live.

Coincidentally he met with the Ramu chacha as he was coming out of that Palace to pour water from the pond.

Ramu chacha - Who are you ? I didn't see you here before.

Godse - Yes, my name is Detective Godse and I came here for the investigation of the mysterious case of this place "Kollapur".

Ramu chacha - oh.

Suddenly a man driving a Thar (One of the most expensive cars) came to me and said to Ramu chacha "Who is he ?"

Ramu chacha - He is detective Godse and he came here for the investigation of the Mysterious case of this place.

That man said look my name is Raghu, the Don of this place, so be careful of me and better to go home without solving this case or your body will also die and by saying this he moved on.

Ramu chacha - I am sorry from my side for this rude behaviour.How he became so rich from a beggar in these 4 months ?God knows ?

Suddenly a call came in Godse's phone. Ring, ring.

Godse - Yes what happened ?

Phone lady - are you Mr Godse ?

Godse - Yes.

Phone lady - you booked a room in a hotel in Kolhapur but I am sorry to say thatThe booking got canceled.

Godse - what a pleasant surprise? and end up the call in anger.

Ramu chacha - Don't worry you can stay in this palace with me .

Godse - Today is my bad luck as well as good luck.

Godse - Thank you very much.

The plot shifted at night

Godse was studying about the case by reading the documents of the case in that palace. In this 4 months 10 people died and 16 people disappeared mysteriously and his doubt goes to Raghu who was the don of this area.After that Ramu Chacha came from the kitchen to his room to give him a cup of tea.

Godse - Achcha why this palace is known as a haunted Palace ?

Ramu Chacha - A long time ago Deva Chandra who was the owner of this Chandra Kateera Palace and the richest person of this place had two sons, one named Abhi Chandra and another named Bala Chandra. Deva Chandra had a very expensive diamond. During the last minutes of Deva Chandra's life, Deva Chandra gave the Diamond to Bala Chandra due to this Abhi Chandra got jealous and planned to kill Bala Chandra and he was successful in killing Bala Chandra and after that he took the Diamond with him and went to foreign.After that spirit of Bala Chandra moved in this palace and kill those people who are mainly the Businessman who pass the street near the palace at 1:00 AM.He also saw the photos of Deva Chandra, Abhi Chandra but he didn't have the picture of Bala Chandra.

Godse - Did you know Ramu Chacha when the new Businessman will come again ?

Ramu Chacha - I think today ?

Godse - Oh that's great.

At 1:00 a.m,When everyone was sleeping, Godse came out from that palace and went to Raghu's house with police.

One of the policemen broke Raghu's house door and entered his house and there they found that Raghu was sleeping.

Suddenly the Police inspector got a call and in that call another police officer was talking that the businessman who was going to pass the street near the palace had disappeared.

Godse - How could it be possible ? Means the killer is another guy.

The police got ferocious on Godse.

One of the policemen said that Godse is not capable of being a detective.

Police Inspector - A waste of time.

Godse was very sad and came to the palace again with disappointment.

CHAPTER SEVEN

MYSTERY OF KOLLAPUR PART - 2

Next morning police found the Businessman to be dead who had disappeared yesterday and his body floating on the pond.

Godse started doing more study on this case .

Ramu Chacha - Oh ! babu do not take this much stress about this case be cool take some break,have your breakfast.

Godse - Case is more important than breakfast.

Godse May the plan to catch a killer. He will spread fake news among the people of this place that today also a new businessman is coming to pass the street near the Palace at 1:00 a.m. and at 1:00 a.m. he will pretend to be a businessman by wearing the costume of a businessman and by this technique he will catch the killer.

According to this plan, Godse did the same thing.At 1:00 a.m. he went to that street by wearing the Businessman costume and pretending to be a businessman.

While he was working on the street he felt someone present behind him so he turned his head backward to see if anyone was there and when he again turned his head forward , he saw a lady wearing a white cloth.She has long straight dirty hair and coming very fast towards me in a creepy manner.

He became scared and started chanting Hanuman Chalisa.

When the lady was close to him, he realized that the lady wearing the hair was fake and it was a mask. So, he grabs the head of that lady and pulls it out saying Jai Sri Ram.

When he pulled the mask out ,his mind blew up.

As it was the Ramu Chacha behind this lady ghost.

Ramu chacha in a creepy voice told him the truth that Deva Chandra gave the expensive diamond to Abhi Chandra not to Bala Chandra and Bala Chandra became jealous and planned to kill his brother but while killing him, Abhi Chandra threw the Diamond into the pond but unfortunately Balachandra killed Abhi Chandra and in reality the Bala Chandra is the Ramu chacha and in present time Ramu chacha have a bad economic condition so he started to killing the Businessman as a name of Abhi Chandra's spirit who passed the street near the palace and took the expensive things from them and from those things he afford his needs of day to day life.

Fourth Wall Breaks

Godse - I know it sounds very sad but a killer is always a killer so he has to get the punishment.

Godse - Am I right or wrong ?

Come to the Plot

The police arrested Ramu chacha.

Finally , Godse completed this case before 7 days by solving it so he will get a promotion with extra payments so,he became very proud of himself.

Credit Scene

I took my luggage on my back and got on the train to go home.

When I sat on my seat from the window the crematorium of Kolhapur could be seen and there I noticed a Supernatural thing that blew up my mind.

I Saw Abhi Chandra saying thank you to me by doing namaskar to me In that crematorium.

I rubbed my eyes again to see there but there was no one .

I think it is my hallucination.

I also saw the Sadhu who was sitting on a bench of that station and was smiling at me and at that time I felt very ecstatic.

Mid - Credit Scene

When I was passing the Nilgum station, I saw Jonathan , Raju and Ravi standing outside the station.

Post Credit Scene

After reaching my department and Boss's room again my boss said "Well done, I know you can do that".

Boss - look I have a gift for you.

Godse - what sir ?

Boss - At first introduce him, he is Vikram Kumar and from now he will be your assistant .

Godse - Are you brave ?

Vikram - Braveness is in our blood. I am brave like my father as my father was a police inspector.

Godse - Oh! What is the name of your father ?

Vikram - Akhil Kumar.

Godse - Oh ! So, his father spread the news among the villagers that Anil meant Jonathan, the new station master, was a serial killer.

Vikram - Did you say anything Sir ?

Godse - Nothing .

Boss - There is a new case for you both of them. It is also one of the most dangerous cases ever.

Godse - What case sir ?

Vikram - what is the name of this case ?

Boss -" The Mysterious case of Berreckpore ".

Godse - So are you ready for thc adventurous journey to Berreckpore .

Vikram - I am always ready .

Godse - That's great so, let's go.

9 798889 866305

Printed by Libri Plureos GmbH in Hamburg,
Germany